Characters in th

In order of appearar

Vishnu (VISH-n

In Hinduism, Vishnu is the Preser
He exists alongside Brahma the Creator and Shiva
These three deities are all aspects of Brahman, the Ultimate Reality.

Ravana (RAH-vah-nah)
The Demon King of Lanka

King Dashratha (DAHSH-rah-thah)
King of Ayodhya

Rama (RAH-mah)
The son of King Dashratha,
and the hero of the *Ramayana*

Lakshmana (LAHK-shma-nah)
Rama's younger brother

Sita (SEE-tah)
The daughter of King Janaka,
and the heroine of the *Ramayana*

King Janaka (JAHN-ah-kah)
King of Mithila

Kaikeyi (KAI-kay-ee)
King Dashratha's second wife,
mother of Bharata

Jatayu (JUH-tie-ew)
King of the Birds

Hanuman (HUH-noo-mahn)
God of the Wind

To the memory of my father, on whose lap I first heard the *Ramayana* under the Nairobi night sky — J. V.

For Sarwat — N. M.

Barefoot Books
2067 Massachusetts Ave
Cambridge, MA 02140

Barefoot Books
29/30 Fitzroy Square
London, W1T 6LQ

First published in the United Kingdom by Barefoot Books, Ltd
and in the United States of America by Barefoot Books, Inc
in 2002 as *The Story of Divaali*
This revised edition first published in 2016

Graphic design by Sarah Soldano, Barefoot Books and Judy Linard, London
Reproduction by Bright Arts, Singapore
Printed in China on 100% acid-free paper
This book was typeset in Minion, Dalliance and Present
The illustrations were prepared in gouache on 140lb watercolor paper

ISBN 978-1-78285-307-7

Library of Congress Cataloging-in-Publication Data
is available under LCCN 2002000204

British Cataloguing-in-Publication Data: a catalogue record
for this book is available from the British Library

1 3 5 7 9 8 6 4 2

The Story of Diwali

retold by
Jatinder Verma

illustrated by
Nilesh Mistry

Contents

Chapter One
A Prince Appears

In the beginning, long ago, long before you were born, Vishnu, Preserver of the Universe, lay asleep on his giant hooded cobra. His booming snores created the rising and falling of the tides in the oceans and the rising and setting of the sun in the skies.

One day a humming and popping noise like a swarm of bees buzzed around his head, disturbing his sleep. He tossed this way and that, trying to make the noise go away. When it did not, he first opened one eye to see what the trouble was, then the other. There in front of him were 3,333 gods, all talking at once.

"Oh, great Vishnu," cried the gods, "while you have been sleeping, darkness has crept upon the earth. It is Ravana, the Demon King of Lanka. His pride and his boasting that he is better than all the gods put together has eclipsed the joyful brightness of the sun. Yes, Ravana's breath has eclipsed the sun. You must go down to Earth or soon the heavens themselves will be dark."

Vishnu bowed his head, and when he looked up, there was a twinkle in his eye. He quickly began to form a plan to teach Ravana a lesson. "Tell me," he said, "Is there anyone on Earth who is, at this very moment, making sacrifices to the gods for good fortune?"

"Dashratha!" cried the 3,333 gods. "King Dashratha of Ayodhya is performing a huge sacrifice to plead for a son."

"Very well," said Vishnu. "I shall appear in human form as the son Dashratha has longed for. Ravana will not expect me to challenge him as a mortal."

Then Vishnu closed his eyes, and at that instant became a whirling column of fire. And the fire began to move down, down, down until it hit the ground where King Dashratha was performing his sacrifice. And when the fire touched the ground, there arose through the flames the most handsome prince imaginable, with an immense bow slung on his right shoulder and a single arrow in his left hand.

The prince stepped out of the fire, bowed his head before King Dashratha and, touching his feet, said, "Father, I am Rama, your eldest son." The king looked speechlessly at the miraculous young man, whose body shone as if flames danced upon his skin through powers given to him by Vishnu.

After a moment, Dashratha asked nervously, "You call yourself my eldest son. Does that mean I will have more?"

"You have three wives," said Rama. "I am the son of your eldest wife. Your other wives will each also have a son — Bharata will be my second brother and Lakshmana my youngest." In that moment, Rama's brothers, Lakshmana and Bharata, appeared. Rama embraced each one of them as if they had known each other for an eternity.

King Dashratha was in a daze of happiness, but his priest soon brought him to consider other important matters of the kingdom.

He turned to the king and said, "Your Majesty, your son must have a wife, for he is to become king in his own right one day."

"A wife? Whatever for?" the king asked. "While the whole world is covered in darkness by the strutting pride of Ravana, what would a wife bring?"

"My king," replied the wise priest, "your son Rama is born of fire, but in order to rule his kingdom justly and mercifully he will need a companion, a woman born of the earth, who can balance the fire from which Rama is made."

The king then asked the high priest who would make a suitable wife for his son Rama. "The beautiful Princess Sita, daughter of King Janaka," said the high priest immediately. "She is the woman your son needs by his side. Rama will bring to her light and warmth, while she will provide Rama with the love and support he needs to rule wisely and well."

And so Prince Rama set off straight away for the kingdom of Mithila, where King Janaka ruled.

Chapter Two

The Contest

When Rama and the high priest reached the the court of King Janaka, they found themselves in the midst of a crowd of hundreds and thousands of handsome young noblemen. Each one had come, like Rama, to bid for the hand of the beautiful Princess Sita. When Sita set her eyes on Rama, she knew at once that this was the man she wanted to marry. As for Rama, he fell in love instantly, and knew that he must take Sita home as his bride.

King Janaka silenced the crowd that had gathered from all corners of the world and announced, "Here before you lies the great bow of Shiva the Destroyer. First, with your left hand, you must lift it up. And then, you must string it. And then you must set this great arrow, also given to me by Shiva the Destroyer, on the bowstring. Then, without looking at it directly, you must shoot the arrow straight into the eye of the fish that spins on the wheel set high above our heads. He among you who can do all these things will prove he is not only skilled enough but also has the necessary sureness of purpose to be a worthy husband for my beloved daughter."

At his words a murmur rose in the great hall. Some of the young men bowed their heads and turned away because the challenge King Janaka had set was too difficult. Others puffed out their chests and strode up to the bow of Shiva, expecting to be able to lift it easily.

One by one, each fell flat on his back without moving the bow even an inch. And so the day wore on, and the bow lay unmoved at Princess Sita's feet.

All of a sudden, there was a tremendous thunderclap; the sky darkened, and there in the doorway to Janaka's palace stood Ravana, the Demon King of Lanka. Without a word, he strode through the palace, scattering the crowd as he went. He glanced once at Princess Sita, who returned his look with curiosity, as if wondering how he would fare. Ravana bent down to lift the great bow of Shiva. It did not budge. With a furious bellow that shook the palace he tried again and fell smack on his face to the ground. A great shout of laughter burst through the hall. Even Sita could not help but laugh at how the proud Ravana had fallen. Her laugh did not go unnoticed. As he picked himself up, Ravana turned to her and growled, "A day will come when laughter will become a stranger to you, Princess Sita!" And, muttering horribly, the Demon King of Lanka stormed out.

Rama could contain himself no longer. "I am born of Vishnu," he thought to himself. "I must end this contest now and prove to Sita and all of the kingdom that I am the man she should marry."

Prince Rama stood up, and without taking his eyes from Sita's face, lifted the great bow with his left hand, strung it effortlessly and shot the arrow straight into the middle of the eye of the fish circling overhead.

Sita laughed in joy, and a roar of applause filled the hall of King Janaka. "I have made laughter your friend again, Princess Sita," said Rama.

Sita picked up a garland of flowers from the gold tray lying beside her, and, placing it around Rama's neck, said, "If laughter is our constant companion, this marriage will prove heaven made."

"And so it is," declared King Janaka, and from the roof of the great hall, hundreds and thousands of sweet-smelling jasmine petals fell to the floor. Sita looked at Rama, and when he returned her look with a smile as wide as the teeming ocean, she felt that her sorrow at the prospect of leaving her father's home for a new life with Rama was completely relieved.

Rama was sure this was the beginning of an adventure he would never grow tired of. He was eager for the chance to learn everything about his new bride.

When Rama returned to Ayodhya with Sita as his bride, the entire kingdom was filled with festivities welcoming the resplendent young couple. It was as if the sun bathed every step the newlyweds took with warm light.

Chapter Three

The Promise

Not everyone was happy about the marriage of Rama and Sita. In a shadowy state room in the palace, there was one who sat brooding, a dark cloud glowering over her head — this was Rama's stepmother, King Dashratha's second wife, Kaikeyi.

Kaikeyi sulked alone in her room. "Now that Rama has a wife," she brooded, "a son will follow soon. And when that happens, my own son, Bharata, will lose the chance of becoming king of Ayodhya. It is a mother's duty to get the best for her son, and I would fail in my duty if I did not try to make sure my own Bharata becomes king."

Kaikeyi sent for King Dashratha. So exhilarated was he at his son's wedding that, on seeing his queen sitting alone, he said, "My queen, why this long face? Come, ask me for anything you desire and it will be yours! For today is a day like no other! Come, let me make you even happier than I am today."

"Do you promise?" asked Kaikeyi.

"I promise what I say will come to pass," replied Dashratha. "So come, my queen, tell me how I can make you happy."

So Kaikeyi told King Dashratha that her son Bharata, not Rama, had to become king after Dashratha, and that Rama must be sent away into exile for fourteen years.

When Dashratha heard these words, his heart turned to stone, and he collapsed on the floor. Rama rushed into the room and, seeing his father lying on the floor, looked up at Kaikeyi in horror.

"He made me a promise. Now he wants to take it back," said his stepmother.

"I will fulfill any promise made by my father," replied Rama with dignity.

"Then you must leave for the forest immediately, so that my son Bharata may become king." A gleam of malice sparkled in Kaikeyi's eyes as she spoke.

Rama turned to Dashratha, who was now weeping. "Father," said Rama, "please don't be sad. I am proud to carry out your promise. Sons are born to obey their parents, so let joy fill your heart again, knowing that the word you have given will not be broken."

So Rama left the palace of Dashratha. As he walked through the city gates, he heard soft footsteps behind him and the sweet voice of Sita saying, "Rama, my husband, how can you think of leaving without me? I am the companion of your days, and wherever your fate leads, mine leads too."

Moments later, Lakshmana, Rama's younger brother, ran up. "You cannot go without me!" he cried breathlessly. "It is a brother's duty to help his brother." So all three of them continued on their way.

The news of Dashratha's promise to Kaikeyi had spread fast: thousands of citizens, young and old, put down their work and came out onto the streets to watch the young people as they set out on their journey. Everyone stood in respectful silence, quietly mourning their exile. At last, Rama, Sita and Lakshmana left the city and came to the bank of the great River Ganges, where a boatman ferried them across the water. As the boat took them farther and farther away from Ayodhya, a hush now fell over them, watching their glittering home disappear on the horizon and the forest of Dandaka rise ahead, dark and full of mystery.

Chapter Four
The Golden Deer

Sita turned to Rama and said, "We have left one life and are about to begin another. We must change our clothes." Rama and Lakshmana stripped bark from the trees, which Sita made into clothes for the three of them. All their jewelry, their fine silks and other garments that they had worn as princes and princesses of a great kingdom, they gave to the boatman as payment for his services.

When they came upon a clearing in the forest, Sita suggested they build a small hut made of bark and cover it with banana leaves. This simple hut became their new home, where each had a task to do. Every morning, Rama and Lakshmana would leave the hut to hunt for food, while Sita gathered berries and herbs. Sita also made friends with the small animals and birds that roamed nearby, and they repaid her kindness by becoming trustworthy guardians of the trio's new home. Where once they had had hundreds of servants to look after their every need, now they had only themselves. But all three of them enjoyed this new adventure, not missing for a single day the pleasures of the palace they had been forced to leave. Thus, the years passed.

One day, when Rama and Lakshmana had returned from their morning's hunting, and the three friends were just finishing the first meal of the day, Sita saw a little golden deer eating leaves from a small bush. She let out a sigh of longing and admiration.

Turning to Rama she said, "Have you ever seen an animal more exquisite? Oh, Rama, please bring that deer to me! When the two of you go out hunting together, I am all alone. This deer will be my companion."

Rama was worried each time he left Sita alone to go hunting. And now, the sudden appearance of this golden deer made him suspicious. But he could not refuse Sita. Picking up his bow and arrow, Rama told Lakshmana to stay behind with Sita while he went to catch the deer.

As Rama drew close to the deer, it turned abruptly and leapt over the bush, running deep into the forest. Rama gave chase, running as fast as he could. Soon, both of them were hidden from the eyes of Sita and Lakshmana. As Rama chased the deer, he found that whenever he drew near, it would slip away. Deeper and deeper into the forest the deer took Rama, until even the sun could not send its rays through the leaves. At last, Rama grew tired of the chase. He picked up his bow and shot an arrow, aiming to wound the creature's leg and slow it down. Just as the arrow struck the deer, a voice that sounded exactly like Rama's rang out through the forest: "Sita, Sita! Help me! Lakshmana, come quickly!"

Sita heard the cry and said, "Lakshmana! Rama is hurt! We must go and help him!" but Lakshmana refused.

"That is not Rama's true voice," he answered. "The deer was a demon sent to trick us into leaving."

But Sita wouldn't give him any peace. "If you won't come with me to help him, then I'll go on my own!"

Lakshmana glared at her. "Very well, I'll go and chase your illusion — but I have one condition." Saying that, Lakshmana paused for a moment. He withdrew an arrow from his quiver and, praying fervently to Vishnu, drew a circle on the ground around the hut. "Whatever you do," he told Sita, "you must not step outside this circle. As long as you stay inside this circle, you will be under the protection of Vishnu. That way, no harm will come to you, and I can still obey Rama's command."

Sita nodded. "I give you my word that I shall stay inside the circle," she said. "Go quickly and help Rama. You do not need to worry about me." Then Lakshmana ran off into the forest.

Chapter Five

King of the Birds

Lakshmana's departure did not go unnoticed. Within minutes, an old man appeared near the hut. Dressed in torn and dirty clothes, he could hardly stand, and had to support himself on a crooked stick. "Is anyone there?" he called. "Help! Please help me." Sita came out of the hut and greeted the old man. "How hungry I am," moaned the old man, "and so tired and thirsty too. Is there any food to eat in the house, and water to drink?"

Quickly Sita went back into the hut and brought out a bowl of rice and a pot of water. The old man stepped forward, but as his foot crossed the line Lakshmana had drawn on the ground, a huge wall of flame rose from the ground, encircling the hut. The old man fell back, crying that he had only asked for some food to eat. "I am

tired, so tired," said the old man. "I will wait here. Bring the food to me if you have pity on me, daughter, or leave me to die."

Holding the bowl of rice in one hand and the pot of water in the other, Sita bowed her head in shame. "I promised Lakshmana that I would not step over this circle," she thought, "but this is only a tired and hungry old man. How can I not help him?" With that thought, she stepped outside the circle.

In a flash, the old man turned into Ravana, the Demon King of Lanka. He grabbed Sita by her wrist.

"Let me go!" shouted Sita.

"You laughed at me at your wedding — now I will rob you of that laughter," shouted Ravana.

"Never! I will never let you steal my soul!" said Sita angrily, but Ravana had a tight hold of her wrist. He dragged her into his winged chariot and flew off into the sky. The sun, which had been shining gently a few moments ago, suddenly clouded over, and darkness fell upon Dandaka Forest.

Ravana's chariot rose higher and higher through the dark clouds. As it sped across the skies to his palace in Lanka, a huge vulture flew up to challenge its driver. This was Jatayu, King of the Birds, whose wings ran the length of the sky. "Help me, Jatayu! Help me get back to Rama!" shouted Sita. Jatayu lashed out at the chariot with just the tip of one wing, forcing Ravana to slow down.

There followed a fierce fight, for Ravana was quick to draw his mighty sword. But when he raised it

to strike at one of Jatayu's wings, Sita pulled back his arm — only for Ravana to shove her back, throwing her to the floor of the chariot. Enraged, Jatayu dove at Ravana, striking him with a mighty swish of one of his wings.

"Do not harm Sita!" he thundered. "Release her, or you will die, for you have no right to carry her away from here!" Ravana took no notice. Then, with his wings spread out wide, Jatayu swooped once more.

But the Demon King quickly slashed Jatayu's wings. One! Two! The battle was over. Without his wings, the great Jatayu fell slowly from the sky, down through the dark clouds. Ravana laughed horribly as he continued his journey to Lanka with Sita still his prisoner.

Jatayu fell with a crash into Dandaka Forest, close to Sita's hut. There it was that Rama and Lakshmana came upon the vulture. "Rama, Rama," said the dying Jatayu,"Ravana tricked you with the golden deer. He has taken Sita to Lanka. Forgive me, Rama, I could not save her."

"There is nothing to forgive, Jatayu," Rama said. "You have done more than we could. And you have paid a greater price than we would have wished. You will live long in my heart, Jatayu."

Then Jatayu breathed his last and died.

"It was my fault. I should never have left her!" cursed Lakshmana.

"Words are useless now," said Rama.

"We must find Sita. Tear down the hut and we'll set off."

"Can we two, by ourselves, defeat Ravana and his army of demons and win Sita back?" asked Lakshmana, his voice full of doubt.

Rama did not answer. He gathered his weapons, and the two brothers began to walk south through the forest.

Chapter Six

Hanuman's Monkey Army

For many days and nights, the brothers hurried on, until one day they came to a clearing — and there, standing in front of them, was their brother Bharata. "Rama, I beg you, please return to Ayodhaya," said Bharata with tears in his eyes. "Our father has died!" As the words passed Bharata's lips, it was as if the forest itself mourned.

"No!" Rama's cry pierced the air in the forest, echoing from tree to tree, as he fell to his knees.

"When my mother tried to place the crown on my head, I refused it. I swore to all our people that Ayodhya had a new king, and that he was Rama," continued Bharata.

"I will not return until Sita walks beside me," said Rama. "Go back and rule in my stead."

"Then give me your sandals," said Bharata. "I will place them on the throne at Ayodhya so everyone can see I rule on your behalf."

Rama gave Bharata his sandals, and together with Lakshmana he continued on through the dense forest. One evening, they found themselves walking along a narrow deer path. Looking ahead, they saw a huge, old monkey lying across the track.

"We must pay our respects," Rama told Lakshmana.

"Respect? *Him?*" Lakshmana cried out indignantly.

"Yes," said Rama, "for this old monkey you see before you can be none other than Ayodhya's oldest friend and ally, who has looked after our kingdom throughout the ages. He is Hanuman, God of the Wind."

As soon as Rama said his name, the old monkey vanished, and in his place stood the mighty Hanuman, sixty feet tall and carrying a huge golden mace. Hanuman knelt on one knee and, pressing his palms together, bowed before Rama. "It is not for Rama and Lakshmana to bow before Hanuman, but for Hanuman to pay his respects to the great princes of Ayodhya! Forgive me for my little trick, but I wanted to make sure you were indeed Rama and Lakshmana and not some demons in disguise. But tell me, what are you doing here?"

The brothers told him all that had happened to them, and that they were going to Lanka to bring Sita back. "You have a long journey ahead of you," Hanuman told them, "for Ravana's kingdom in Lanka is an island that lies miles away from the edge of the forest, surrounded by deep ocean. Perhaps I can make your search easier. Come, I will take you both to the edge of the forest, so you can see for yourselves." So saying, Hanuman lifted Rama and Lakshmana onto his shoulders, jumped high into the sky and flew like the wind to the edge of Dandaka Forest.

When they reached the edge of the forest, they could all see the island of Lanka in the far distance, with the roaring sea between them. Fires burned all over the island, and smoke rose high from these fires, clouding the light of the sun. Rama was at a loss. "How can we get across?' he asked out loud. "And how can the two of us take on the ten thousand demons of Ravana's army?"

By way of an answer, Hanuman whistled out loud, and the sound was like the crack of thunder. A moment later, from the shore behind them, there arose a noise like waves in the sea, getting louder as it grew nearer. Soon, lined up on the shore, there stood thousands and thousands of monkeys. "Here," said Hanuman, "is the answer to both your worries! Our Monkey Army will gather all the stones from Dandaka Forest and build a bridge across the sea. We shall use big stones, small stones, any stones we can find, and we shall join this place marked by your feet with the island that lies smoking on the horizon!"

"Excellent," said Rama, "now we have numbers to match Ravana's army. But remember, Ravana's powers are almost equal to Vishnu's. The Demon King of Lanka cannot easily be defeated. Let us build the bridge quickly, but we must keep a watchful eye on any tricks Ravana may play."

And so, Hanuman and his Monkey Army began to work, building their bridge over the ocean to Lanka. Seven times the sun rose in the east and sank in the west, and on the eighth day, the bridge was complete.

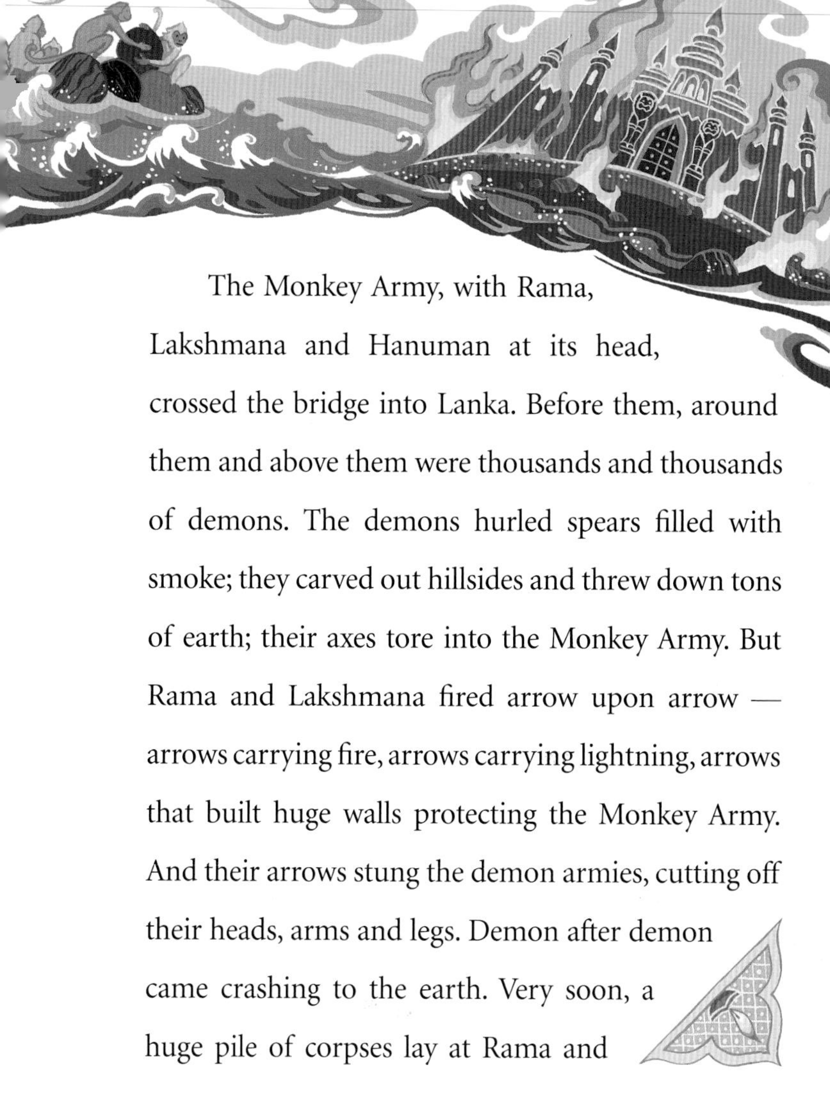

The Monkey Army, with Rama, Lakshmana and Hanuman at its head, crossed the bridge into Lanka. Before them, around them and above them were thousands and thousands of demons. The demons hurled spears filled with smoke; they carved out hillsides and threw down tons of earth; their axes tore into the Monkey Army. But Rama and Lakshmana fired arrow upon arrow — arrows carrying fire, arrows carrying lightning, arrows that built huge walls protecting the Monkey Army. And their arrows stung the demon armies, cutting off their heads, arms and legs. Demon after demon came crashing to the earth. Very soon, a huge pile of corpses lay at Rama and

Lakshmana's feet. It seemed that all the demons that had ever frightened anyone in the world were dying, so fierce was the battle.

At last, Ravana came storming out of his palace. "Come and fight me, Rama! Fight me if you dare! I will not fall as easily as my demons. Sita is mine, and from this day, when I finally defeat you, this world will know only darkness. Dark clouds will rob smiles from all faces, and people will hide from the light! Come and fight me if you dare!"

Before Rama could take up the challenge, Lakshmana put an arrow in his

bow and let it fly at the sneering Ravana. Sita, watching the battle from her prison high in Ravana's towering palace, willed Lakshmana's arrow to strike Ravana dead. She saw the sharp arrowhead tear into his neck — but as soon as Ravana's face fell silent, another grew in its place, mocking Lakshmana! She saw Lakshmana fire arrow upon arrow, holding her breath each time — nine times Lakshmana's arrows struck Ravana's neck, and nine times a new face arose, laughing so loud the earth shook to the skies. The hope that had risen in Sita's heart when the fight had begun now drained away.

"Is that the best you can do?" shouted Ravana. "Is this the limit of your power to save Sita? Don't hide behind your brother, Rama! Come out and face me alone."

When he heard Ravana's boasts, Rama blazed with fury. Wild flames danced on his skin, and his eyes gleamed as he stooped to place his best arrow in his great bow. Just then, Hanuman came up to him. "Rama," murmured Hanuman, "you are mistaken if you think Ravana's power lies in his head. Aim your arrow — the arrow you won long ago in King Janaka's palace — aim that arrow into Ravana's stomach, for that is where the seat of his power lies."

Then Rama calmed himself, bowed in prayer before his arrow and, stringing it to his bow, let

The Festival of Light

By the time they drew near to Ayodhya, night had fallen. Sita suddenly cried out, "Rama, look — look below! All those shining lights! It's as if the stars have moved from the heavens above to the earth below!"

"Fair Sita," Hanuman explained, "your return is not a surprise to the citizens of Ayodhya. They have all lit oil lamps in their windows to celebrate your homecoming, and to show their love and respect for their new king and queen.

Ayodhya rejoices, and every man, woman, child and elder welcomes you. The vaults full of ghee and butter are open; the fountains are sparkling. The flowers are in full bloom, and the musicians are ready, for tonight will be a special night for everyone alive."

"Diwali," murmured Rama.

"Diwali?" asked Sita.

"A festival of lights," said Rama. "From this day forward, for all time to come,

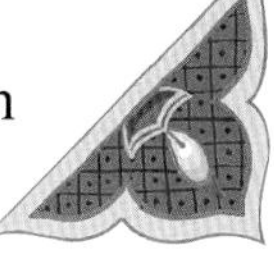

this special night will be remembered in just this way all over the world — the night that Rama and Sita returned home!"

Then Hanuman landed in the palace courtyard among the joyful citizens of Ayodhya, and everyone burst into song. And when Rama, Sita and Lakshmana felt again the earth of their home beneath their feet, night suddenly turned into day and from the shining sun, it seemed, hundreds and thousands of sweet-smelling jasmine petals fell down to Earth.

The Festival of Diwali

Diwali (dih-WAH-lee) is a major Hindu festival, similar in significance to holidays like Christmas, Hanukkah and Eid. It lasts for five days, starting on the new moon night of the Hindu month of Kartika, which usually falls in October or November. The festival is marked in households, shops and public places by small oil lamps (called "diwa" in Hindi) lined up on window ledges and along doorways. Firework displays have become customary accompaniments to the festival, with rockets and sparklers being the most common. Diwali is also a social occasion, when families gather and gifts and sweetmeats are exchanged with relatives and friends.

In Indian cities, and wherever else in the world that Indians live, Diwali turns night into day, with electric light bulbs replacing diwas where necessary. Although essentially a Hindu festival, in India it is not uncommon for it to be celebrated by Muslims, Christians, Buddhists, Sikhs and Jains. Like the triumph of Rama and Sita over the Demon King, Ravana, Diwali celebrates the victory of light over darkness, good over evil, hope over despair. It also marks the start of the Hindu New Year, so it is a time when people clean their houses and offices, ready for a new start. It is considered especially bad luck to turn away a stranger who comes to the door during Diwali.

Diwali is the time when businessmen and women balance their accounts, hoping that Lakshmi, the Goddess of Wealth, will grace them in the year to come. Those who have no accounts to do celebrate the occasion by gambling! In many parts of northern India, Diwali is also the occasion for a particular form of street drama, called Raam-Lila (literally, the "Play of Rama"). Children and adults often prepare throughout the year for this reenactment of the story of Rama and Sita. Elaborate costumes are made and sets erected, transforming local sites into settings for the Diwali story. Typically, children are chosen to play Rama, Sita and Lakshmana and, throughout the period of the presentation, these children are revered by all as the incarnations of these three deities.

The story of Diwali, the *Ramayana* (rah-mai-AH-nah), was composed by the poet Valmiki as an epic poem — like the ancient English *Beowulf* and the Greek *Odyssey* — around the 5th century B. C. E. It has since been handed down through the oral tradition for many centuries, in addition to being rewritten by other poets, with many variants and side stories surrounding the central plot. Like any son or daughter of India, my introduction to this great epic was through my parents. My father shared the adventures of Rama and Sita with me when I was a child, and his influence was reinforced by my mother's frequent recitations of the version that is best known in north India today — that of the 16th-century poet Tulsidas. My retelling is based on Valmiki and Tulsida's versions as well as my father's stories.

Jatinder Verma